Children's Folklore

North American Folklore

Children's Folklore
Christmas and Santa Claus Folklore
Contemporary Folklore
Ethnic Folklore
Family Folklore
Firefighters' Folklore
Folk Arts and Crafts
Folk Customs
Folk Dance
Folk Fashion
Folk Festivals
Folk Games
Folk Medicine
Folk Music
Folk Proverbs and Riddles
Folk Religion
Folk Songs
Folk Speech
Folk Tales and Legends
Food Folklore
Regional Folklore

North American Folklore

Children's Folklore

BY SHERRY BONNICE

Mason Crest Publishers

Mason Crest Publishers Inc.
370 Reed Road
Broomall, Pennsylvania 19008
(866) MCP-BOOK (toll free)
www.masoncrest.com

First printing
1 2 3 4 5 6 7 8 9 10
Library of Congress Cataloging-in-Publication Data on file at the Library of Congress.
ISBN 1-59084-329-0
　　　1-59084-328-2 (series)

Design by Lori Holland.
Composition by Bytheway Publishing Services, Binghamton, New York.
Cover design by Joe Gilmore.
Printed and bound in the Hashemite Kingdom of Jordan.

Picture credits:
Comstock: pp. 14, 18, 30, 38, 54, 59, 60, 61, 62, 86, 97, 98, 100
Eclectic Collections: pp. 16, 20, 50, 68, 78, 90, 92
Eyewire: p. 82
PhotoDisc: pp. 6, 8, 10, 11, 13, 22, 24, 25, 26, 27, 31, 32, 33, 34, 36, 40, 43, 44, 46,
　　　　47, 49, 52, 56, 58, 62, 66, 71, 72, 80, 84, 87, 88, 94, 97
Cover: "Springtime" by Norman Rockwell © 1931 SEPS: Licensed by Curtis Publishing,
　　　Indianapolis, IN. www.curtispublishing.com

　　　Printed by permission of the Norman Rockwell Family
　　　© the Norman Rockwell Family Entities

Contents

Folklore grows from long-ago
seeds. Just as an acorn sends
down roots even as it shoots up
leaves across the sky, folklore is
rooted deeply in the past and
yet still lives and grows today.
It spreads through our modern
world with branches as wide
and sturdy as any oak's;
it grounds us in yesterday even
as it helps us make sense of
both the present and the future.

Introduction

by Dr. Alan Jabbour

WHAT DO A TALE, a joke, a fiddle tune, a quilt, a jig, a game of jacks, a saint's day procession, a snake fence, and a Halloween costume have in common? Not much, at first glance, but all these forms of human creativity are part of a zone of our cultural life and experience that we sometimes call "folklore."

The word "folklore" means the cultural traditions that are learned and passed along by ordinary people as part of the fabric of their lives and culture. Folklore may be passed along in verbal form, like the urban legend that we hear about from friends who assure us that it really happened to a friend of their cousin. Or it may be tunes or dance steps we pick up on the block, or ways of shaping things to use or admire out of materials readily available to us, like that quilt our aunt made. Often we acquire folklore without even fully realizing where or how we learned it.

Though we might imagine that the word "folklore" refers to cultural traditions from far away or long ago, we actually use and enjoy folklore as part of our own daily lives. It is often ordinary, yet we often remember and prize it because it seems somehow very special. Folklore is culture we share with others in our communities, and we build our identities through the sharing. Our first shared identity is family identity, and family folklore such as shared meals or prayers or songs helps us develop a sense of belonging. But as we grow older we learn to belong to other groups as well. Our identities may be ethnic, religious, occupational, or regional—or all of these, since no one has only one cultural identity. But in every case, the identity is anchored and strengthened by a variety of cultural traditions in which we participate and share with our neighbors. We feel the threads of connection with people we know, but the threads extend far beyond our own immediate communities. In a real sense, they connect us in one way or another to the world.

Folklore possesses features by which we distinguish ourselves from each other. A certain dance step may be African American, or a certain story urban, or a certain hymn Protestant, or a certain food preparation Cajun. Folklore can distinguish us, but at the same time it is one of the best ways we introduce ourselves to each other. We learn about new ethnic groups on the North American landscape by sampling their cuisine, and we enthusiastically adopt musical ideas from other communities. Stories, songs, and visual designs move from group to group, enriching all people in the process. Folklore thus is both a sign of identity, experienced as a special marker of our special groups, and at the same time a cultural coin that is well spent by sharing with others beyond our group boundaries.

Folklore is usually learned informally. Somebody, somewhere, taught us that jump rope rhyme we know, but we may have trouble remembering just where we got it, and it probably wasn't in a book that was assigned as homework. Our world has a domain of formal knowledge, but folklore is a domain of knowledge and culture that is learned by sharing and imitation rather than formal instruction. We can study it formally—that's what we are doing now!—but its natural arena is in the informal, person-to-person fabric of our lives.

Not all culture is folklore. Classical music, art sculpture, or great novels are forms of high art that may contain folklore but are not themselves folklore. Popular music or art may be built on folklore themes and traditions, but it addresses a much wider and more diverse audience than folk music or folk art. But even in the world of popular and mass culture, folklore keeps popping up around the margins. E-mail is not folklore—but an e-mail smile is. And college football is not folklore—but the wave we do at the stadium is.

This series of volumes explores the many faces of folklore throughout the North American continent. By illuminating the many aspects of folklore in our lives, we hope to help readers of the series to appreciate more fully the richness of the cultural fabric they either possess already or can easily encounter as they interact with their North American neighbors.

Children from all around the world have a folklore all their own.

ONE

Why Children
Like Traditions

A Sense of Security

Children's folklore offers them security in a world where everyone is bigger than they are.

"THINGS HAVE changed so much since I was young." Adults share this sentiment often, especially when feeling frustrated with something they experience as different from what it was in their childhood. They're right: things do change. But the changes they are talking about are in the outside world; things like cloning animals, rising divorce rates, and suicide bombings were not a part of their generation's headlines. The truth is, however, that inwardly we don't change so readily. The things we count on, like love, forgiveness, belonging, and trust, stay the same. From generation to generation, we need to be in relationships where we can feel safe and valuable.

How do we shape these feelings within families? One important way is by continuing traditions, things that we practice over and over again. Family traditions are begun whenever relatives gather together to talk, to celebrate, to work, or to play. One way families share special times together is by telling stories. Some may be about that great camping trip when Uncle Will hooked a bird's nest for lunch. Or how about when Great-Grandma and Great-Grandpa moved to the United States carrying one set of clothes and Grandma's favorite stew pot? And then there's the story of how Dad spent one whole month building a doghouse for Max who never went inside it. These stories bring a family together and share an intergenerational love that makes children feel connected to the past and future.

You may remember hearing Mom and Aunt Mary reminisce about Gram telling them, "Life's not fair" when they endured some disappointing times. And just last week Gram shared the

Siblings pass along folklore between each other.

same wisdom when you couldn't understand why Jim got picked for the soccer team instead of you. In a situation like that, doesn't it help to know you suffered the same frustrations but also the same support as your mom?

Sayings and anecdotes like these are a part of children's folklore, and so are stories. Every child loves stories.

ONCE there lived a little girl named Too-too-moo. She and her mama lived in a one-

For hundreds of years, many rhymes have kept their basic forms and words. Yet each generation adds their own creativity to an old favorite. What happened fifty years ago in Detroit and yesterday in Philadelphia may be set to a rhyme sung during World War II by girls in New York City, each commenting on conditions in her neighborhood or school. Even McDonald's 1970s television and radio commercials were soon changed by children to render their own messages:

> *McDonald's is your kind of place*
> *Hamburgers in your face*
> *French fries up your nose*
> *Ketchup between your toes*
> *McDonald's is your kind of place*
> *Ain't got no parking space*
> *McDonald's is your kind of place*

room house in a forest. They were very poor but they were also very happy. Except for one thing. A terrible giant came to their little home every day looking for food.

Every morning when Too-too-moo woke up, she fastened her hair in a knot with her long hairpin, and hurried to the woods to help Mama gather firewood and herbs to sell at the village market. When they finished their work, Mama made plain rice for breakfast. She and Too-too-moo ate the rice every morning. But Mama also made a huge pot of sweet porridge with tasty rice flour, coconut milk, and lots of sugar. Too-too-moo and her Mama never tasted the delicious porridge, though, because if the

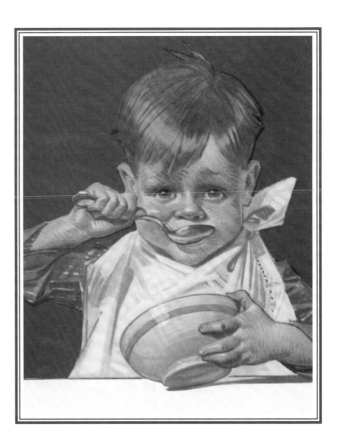

Food has its own childhood folklore.

giant came and didn't find a full pot of porridge he would eat Too-too-moo instead.

After breakfast, Mama left for the market. Too-too-moo stayed home and did the housework. She shook out their sleeping mat, swept the floor, and washed their few dishes. Then she went outside to play.

When she heard the giant's footsteps—BOOM! BOOM! BOOM!—she ran into the house, put the covered pot of porridge on the doorstep, and shut and locked the door. She was very scared as she waited.

The giant came up to the house and yelled, "Too-too-moo! Where are *you?*"

And Too-too-moo answered, "In the house."

"And where is your *mama?*"

"At the market."

"And where is my PORRIDGE?"

"In the pot!"

Then he ate the whole pot of porridge in one big gulp and went back into the forest. This happened every day.

Even when Mama returned with food she bought with that day's earnings there was never enough food for her and Too-too-moo. Mama began selling less at the market and finally could only feed the giant. Too-too-moo and her mama were starving.

According to **folklorists**, the games played by adults with very young children—like patty-cake, horsey, and this-little-piggy—are very nearly the same as they were 300 years ago.

Children from other countries brought their folklore with them to North America.

One morning, when Too-too-moo woke up, she fastened her hair in a knot with her long hairpin, and hurried to the woods to help Mama gather firewood and herbs to sell at the village market. Since Mama only had enough food to make the porridge for the giant, she and Too-too-moo did not eat. When Mama finished making the porridge, she left for the market.

Poor Too-too-Moo, the smell of the porridge was too much for her. She began to take only a spoonful, then another . . . and another . . . until a quarter of the porridge was gone.

When she heard the giant's footsteps—BOOM! BOOM! BOOM!—she covered the pot, put it on the doorstep, and shut and locked the door. She was very scared as she waited.

The giant came up to the house and yelled, "Too-too-moo! Where are *you?*"

And Too-too-moo answered, "In the house."

Folklore is being passed back and forth between children every moment of their days.

"And where is your *mama?*"

"At the market."

"And where is my PORRIDGE?"

"In the pot!"

The giant took off the cover of the pot and looked in, "This pot is not *full!*" he yelled. "Too-too-moo! Where are YOU?"

Too-too-moo did not answer.

The giant knocked down the door, reached into the house, and found Too-too-moo. With one gulp he swallowed her. "Please let me out!" she shouted from the giant's stomach. But he just stamped back into the forest.

Too-too-moo was very scared . . . until she remembered her long hairpin. She took it from her hair and stuck the giant. The giant yelped. She stuck him again. Again he cried out, telling her to stop. But Too-too-moo stuck him again and again. Des-

Fairy tales were originally simply the stories people told each other, things that had happened to someone they knew, amazing events they had heard at the marketplace, or the latest news of political events. Eventually, when fairy tales passed into written literature, they were many times intended for adults, sometimes as political statements. The creation of collections of fairy and folk tales, like the Grimm brothers', reflects a historical change in the way people thought about children. For a long time children had been considered to be just little adults who were taught from adult books and shared in their parents' world. For a short period, they were then viewed as amusing, to the point of being brought into adult gatherings where adults marveled at their antics. Finally, and this *philosophy* exists somewhat still, children were believed to be in need of care and instruction from the adults who had charge of them. Fairy tales provided a part of the instruction by sharing in story form the need to discipline and educate. Themes of honor, truth, obedience, and love reinforce attitudes adults want their children to embody as adults.

perate to escape the pain in his belly, he ran about so wildly that he tripped on a root and hit his head on a rock. The giant was dead!

When Mama returned from the market, she had sold everything that day and bought rice and fish and vegetables, and even roasted peanuts as a special treat for Too-too-moo. Then she saw the porridge pot and porridge thrown on the ground and her mouth turned into a frightened "O." She could not find Too-too-moo.

She called, "Too-too-moo! Where are *you?*" But no one answered.

Mama ran to the forest, following the giant's footsteps, still calling, "Too-too-moo! Where are YOU?"

Long-ago children enjoyed some of the same folklore children do today.

When she found the dead giant, Too-too-moo answered her yells. "I'm in the giant."

Mama opened the giant's mouth wide and out came Too-too-moo.

From that time on, Too-too-moo and her Mama were very happy. They had no giant to feed so they had enough food themselves. And they ate sweet porridge for breakfast, every single day.

YOU may not like sweet porridge—but do you have a favorite food that your mother makes on one of your special days?

Food traditions are a large part of family customs. Christmas cookies, Easter cake, and blueberry pancakes on Dad's birthday are things you will never forget. They will shape the traditions you pass on to your own children.

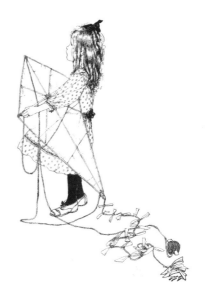

Tradition doesn't only help children to feel safe and happy. It is also an important part of providing children with a moral education. As adults try to impart moral standards, they learn quickly that preaching only turns children away from the sought after results. But through stories, celebrations, prayers, jokes, and songs, parents and grandparents pass along their moral values. Folklore is steeped in *ethical* concepts.

When they hear the tale about Rapunzel and her prince, children love the story even though "the Prince was beside himself with grief, and in his despair he jumped right down from the tower, and, though he escaped with his life, the thorns among which he fell pierced his eyes out. Then he wandered, blind and miserable, through the wood, eating nothing but roots and berries, and weeping and lamenting the loss of his lovely bride." In the end, his sight is restored by the tears of his true love Rapunzel. Children count on good overcoming evil. The ancient fairy-tale traditions continue to survive, because they continue to reassure children. These stories, particularly in their original forms, are not innocent tales for the weak and young; they acknowledge that evil exists and terrible things happen. But in the end, order and goodness are affirmed. When children grow up

Generations of children have created lemonade stands.

hearing these stories, they also absorb a worldview that is ultimately optimistic, creative, and self-confident.

Children's folklore is passed along not through formal education but during times of play and family traditions. All the customs, games, and traditions of childhood add to the child's sense of security. Families provide traditions from the past that influence children today.

Folklore is a way to pass wisdom along from earlier generations.

TWO

Echoes of the Past
Yesterday's Lessons

Family life is the material for the stories that will one day be passed on to yet another generation.

FOLKTALES SEEM to be, on the surface, stories told simply to entertain children. But folktales, especially family folk stories, also allow children to learn how different cultures and values have affected them personally. In most families, children are not only fed and clothed, but in nurturing homes they are also taught about the differences between right and wrong; they are taught to be proud of their family and country's history; and they begin traditions of their own to pass along to their children. Once children make the stories their own and are able to share them with other family members or friends, they become connected to the family or community as a whole.

On a regular basis we share the stories of our lives. Sometimes we relate what happened to us today; other times we share tales of our own or our family's past. These may include legends about local people, our beliefs, and sometimes even jokes that relate to past events. Family members help each other as they move within the home and as they venture out into the world. Home is a proving ground for the task ahead: becoming an individual and living our own lives. Folklore rooted in the past helps children understand who they are in relation to the rest of the world. It gives them both a sense of identity and a sense of belonging.

Many of the stories shared with North American children originated in Native American families who wanted to explain the world around them to their children. Some of this folklore explains why the trees turn colors in the fall or why the bear is so big and the turtle is so slow. These tales help explain natural phenomenon.

Snowball fights are a childhood tradition.

A young Papago girl shared the legend that follows with her classmates.

HOW THE OCEANS CAME TO BE

A long time ago I'itoi, a Great Spirit of the Papago tribe, lived in the world. He knew everything before it happened. One thing he knew was that there was going to be a great flood. The flood would cover the whole earth. He decided to weave a large basket that would float. He sat in the basket and floated around during the flood.

When the flood was over and the earth was still floating in water, he saw that the earth would not stay in one place. I'itoi called the spiders to come and weave great webs that would hold the earth steady. The spiders sewed the earth and the sky together just as I'itoi told them to. Even though they worked very hard, in some places the webs broke from the pressure of the water.

Today we can still see where the webs broke. These are the lakes and the oceans.

Fairy tales are one way that children's folklore is passed along.

SHARING a story of why nature performs the way it does helps children and adults feel a part of the world around them and more importantly a part of each other. Grandma told Dad the story and Great-Grandpa told Grandma. Each learns to look around at the miracles of nature. We realize as we share the earth and its gifts we are all responsible for our actions in dealing with these resources. Native Americans, whether Inuit, Navaho, or Hopi, teach their children a basic love and reverence for the water, air, animals, and plants. Children from other cultures can also learn from these folk traditions.

The past is a tool that folklore allows children to use. Through song and story, the community's past experiences are linked with children's own memories, something they can revisit whenever they are faced with a dilemma. Their personal repertoire of options is enhanced by experiencing the past through folklore. What's more, older generations use folklore to warn children about their world's dangers.

For instance, one family lived near a set of railroad tracks that was in use two or three times a day. Hearing the whistle blow was such a normal part of their day that when cousins came to stay overnight and complained of the loud noise, the family just looked at each other with shrugs. But often when they went out-

Much of what is passed along between the generations occurs unintentionally, without parents ever being aware of what is taking place. Children learn to play by mimicking their parents; for instance, playing house and army have been perennial favorites among kids for years. This sort of play reflects the gender roles of the time; once boys played with trucks or toy guns, while girls played with dolls and toy dishes. Today, children's play offers wider options, just as children will encounter as adults.

Connections to the past. . .

Paintings in Egyptian tombs show children playing ball. Girls were participating in a game similar to jacks well before the birth of Christ. Plato speaks of Greek boys playing Blind Man's Bluff, Hide and Seek, and other games. A hopscotch diagram can still be seen on the pavement of the Roman forum, and Ovid mentions Roman children using polished nuts in a game similar to marbles.

—Mary and Herbert Knapp, *One Potato, Two Potato*

side to play, the mother warned her children not to play on the railroad tracks. "Remember the story of old Mrs. Webber's youngest son. You know the one who limps around town. He's a lucky boy that one. Got away with losing just a part of his foot. Lucky boy. He could have been killed by the train. So don't you play near those tracks."

The kids had heard the story so many times that they barely heard their mother's voice anymore, kind of like the train whistle.

One day the youngest boy came screaming into the house. His hand was completely torn open, and he was bleeding pretty badly.

"What happened to you?" the mother asked as she grabbed dishtowels to cover the gash.

"I fell on a piece of glass," sobbed the young boy.

After a trip to the doctor's and a mess of stitches, the family gathered at the kitchen table for dinner.

"Okay, now I want to hear the story from the beginning," the mother said.

"Well," the older brother began. "We were playing as usual."

"Playing where?" the mother asked.

"You know, around here," the sister stuttered.

"Where around here?" the mother persisted.

Finally, the youngest brother confessed. "Mom, we were on the tracks. I slipped off the rail and. . ."

"On the tracks, huh? I figured as much. Now you'll all go without dessert and tomorrow we'll head over to Grandpa's and you'll hear the whole story about Mrs. Webber's son. I warned you that those tracks were trouble."

Proverbs are another way children learn from the folklore of the past. How many of these did you hear when you were growing up?

If you want your dinner, don't offend the cook.
April showers bring May flowers.
Don't burn your bridges behind you.
Beauty don't boil the pot.
Empty wagons always make the most noise.
Mighty oaks from little acorns grow.
You can't make a silk purse out of a sow's ear.
Rob Peter to pay Paul.
Where there's smoke there's fire.
An ounce of prevention is worth a pound of cure.
Better late than never.
Don't cross your bridges before you come to them.

STORIES about drowning in old fishing holes, children being lost in wooded areas, and terrible accidents crossing busy streets are a part of children's folklore that act as warnings. When we hear about Aunt Pearl's near-death experience ice-skating, we learn a valuable lesson about checking the thickness of the ice before making the choice to ice skate.

Children who are connected to their family's past feel like they belong to a larger family circle. This connection not only re-

inforces values and traditions from the past to the present and into the future, but it also protects family members from one generation to the next.

Although much of children's folklore is handed down from the older generation, probably a larger proportion is passed along between children themselves, from older siblings and classmates to younger children. Relationships between older and younger children may be fraught with rivalry and jealousy, but young children nevertheless learn and grow through these relationships.

If you have brothers and sisters, you've probably noticed that your siblings relate to the world at much the same level as

you. Jokes and little verses that Mom and Dad do not find funny will make your little brother roll on the floor laughing. And the ghost stories your older sister tells you may be far more fascinating than anything Mom comes up with. Chances are, you didn't learn the games you played as a child from either your parents or your teachers—you probably learned them from your siblings or from other children who lived nearby.

Children understand each other. Sometimes they even come to each other's defense.

ONCE long ago there were three billy goats who lived in a meadow. The meadow was at the foot of a mountain. The billy goats were brothers with the last name of Gruff.

One day they decided to go up on the hillside and eat the grass there. "Let's eat and eat and eat, and make ourselves fat," they said to one another.

The youngest brother started out first. He came to a bridge and began to cross. Under the bridge lived a terrible troll. He had huge eyes as big as saucers and a nose as long as a poker that was as crooked as a snake too.

As Smallest Billy Goat Gruff trip-trapped, trip-trapped over the bridge, he heard a loud yell: "Who's that trip-trapping across my bridge?"

Fanciful folktales may contain themes common in real-life families.

Siblings often look out for one another.

"It's only me, the Smallest Billy Goat Gruff," he answered. "I am going up to the hillside to eat some grass."

"I'm going to gobble you up," roared the troll.

"Oh, no, don't eat me. I'm too little. My brother Middle-Sized Billy Goat Gruff will come along soon. He's much bigger than I am."

"Well, you do look very small. Get going," said the troll.

So the Smallest Billy Goat Gruff ran across the bridge trip-trap, trip-trap.

Soon as the Middle-Sized Billy Goat Gruff trip-trapped, trip-trapped over the bridge, he heard a loud yell: "Who's that trip-trapping across my bridge?"

"It's only me, the Middle-Sized Billy Goat Gruff," he answered. "I am going up to the hillside to eat some grass."

"I'm going to gobble you up," roared the troll.

"Oh, no, don't eat me. I'm too little. My brother Big Billy Goat Gruff will come along soon. He's much bigger than I am."

"Well, get going then," said the troll.

Not long after, as Big Billy Goat Gruff trip-trapped, trip-trapped over the bridge, he heard a loud yell: "Who's that trip-trapping across my bridge?"

"It's only me, the Big Billy Goat Gruff," he answered. "I am going up to the hillside to eat some grass."

"I'm going to gobble you up," roared the troll.

"Ha! Ha!" laughed the Big Billy Goat Gruff. "Well, come on, let's get to it. I'm a good fight for any troll."

The troll jumped up onto the bridge. Big Billy Goat Gruff and the troll put their heads down and charged to the center of the bridge. But Big Billy Goat Gruff's head was harder than the troll's. He knocked the troll down and then threw him into the air with his horns. The troll landed in the river below the bridge, never to be seen again.

The memories shared by siblings can forge powerful bonds.

Then the three brothers went up on the hillside where they ate and ate and ate, and made themselves so fat they could hardly walk home.

STORIES with a similar theme are common in folklore. For example, in "The Snow Queen," the sister rescues her brother from the evil witch, and in many other tales, brothers rescue their sister from her lonely enchantment.

Children grow strong with support from each other, from their parents, and from the traditions of the past. Whether in the form of stories, songs, or games, folklore nourishes them with a food that's been cooking for generations.

Children learn to enter the adult world through play.

THREE

Learning to Be Grownup
Children's Play

Often older siblings guide younger children on the path toward adulthood.

Becoming an adult is one of the specific stages of childhood. "I can't wait to be grown up and do whatever I want!" is the battle cry of many pre-teens. Growing up is an important goal, one that leads children on a road that will distance them from their parents and allow them to make the changes they need to become independent, mature adults able to function in their particular society. Folklore provides an outlet for many of the *rites of passage* that occur on the road to maturity.

When socializing among themselves, children share stories, rhymes, and songs that help them through the many physical and emotional changes that occur during these years. Rhymes and scornful remarks from the previous year (for example, "Baby, baby, stick your head in gravy") are often replaced with lore that is more *taboo* and many times a *parody* on what adults try to pass as necessary conduct. (An example of this is this familiar song: "Mine eyes have seen the glory of the burning of the school. . . .") While adults help establish values and goals, teach social principles, and prepare children for independence, children share these lessons with each other by making them their own, many times in ways that adults do not fully understand (and may even find disrespectful).

> *Mine eyes have seen the glory of the burning of the school.*
> *We have tortured every teacher and have broken every rule.*
> *We have hung the principal on the flagpole of the school*
> *As the brats go marching on.*
> *Gory, glory hallelujah, teacher hit me with a ruler.*

I hit her on the bean with a rotten tangerine.
As the brats go marching on.

One of the ways children enjoy declaring their separation from adults is by manipulating some of the old favorite songs or stories. By changing words and ideas, they declare their ability to make an independent decision, one that is different from what adults feel is the **norm**. This is especially true when it comes to school. Teachers and principals represent the authority children are waiting to overcome.

Row, row, row your boat
Gently down the stream
Throw your teacher overboard
And listen to her scream

Subjects that are sensitive often find their way into children's lore. Things like profanity, bodily taboos, and even food habits give children "meat" for a new rhyme, story, or song. Teasing each other about simple things like the foods they eat allows children to think about these habits and **prejudices** away from

USING CHILDREN'S FOLKLORE TO DETERMINE TRUE LOVE

Ice cream soda, lemonade punch,
What's the name of your honeybunch?
A, B, C, . . . (the letter you miss on is your sweetheart's
   initial)

home where other children have differing viewpoints. Breaking table rules or food restrictions in play is just a small way of gaining authority. Even the elaborate clapping and jumping games that go with the rhymes prove the advancement from one stage to the next in maturity.

*On top of spaghetti all covered with cheese
I had a meatball until somebody sneezed*

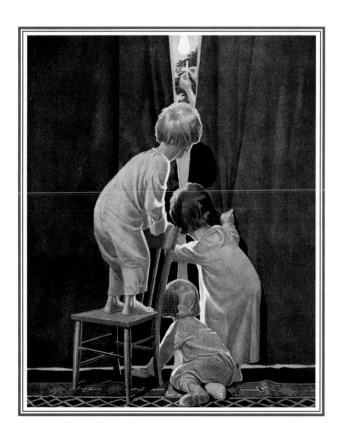

Children are often fascinated by the mysterious adult world.

It rolled onto the table and onto the floor
And my poor meatball rolled out of the door
Into the garden and into a bush
My poor meatball was nothing but mush.
So if you like spaghetti all covered with cheese
Hold onto your meatball when somebody sneeze.

Who cooks the meals is also a question that needs an answer. It used to be that women held that role but not so today. Young men and women need to cope with role reversals that their parents and grandparents did not. Sometimes these thoughts are

acted out in rhymes. Learning gender roles is one of childhood's tasks.

Despite the various tensions between the sexes, the quest for the perfect mate often starts when children are very young. Before they know anything about jobs, heating bills, and mortgages, little girls shout jump-rope rhymes like these:

Gypsy, gypsy, please tell me,
Who my husband is going to be,
Rich man, poor man, beggarman, thief,
Doctor, lawyer, merchant, chief,
Butcher, baker, candlestick maker,
Tinker, tailor, cowboy, sailor.
Gypsy, gypsy, please tell me

Have you jumped rope to this rhyme?

Mary Mack, all dressed in black,
Silver and gold buttons down her back.
Ask her ma for 15 cents
To see the elephant jump the fence.
He jumped so high he touched the sky
And won't come back
Till the Fourth of July.

What my dress is going to be,
Silk, satin, calico, rags.
Gypsy, gypsy, please tell me
What my ring is going to be,
Diamond, ruby, sapphire, glass.

Here's another jump-rope rhymes that focuses on romance:

Cinderella
Dressed in yellow
Went downtown to see her fellow.
On the way her girdle busted.
How many men were disgusted?
One, two, three, four, five. . . .

SPANISH DANCER

(a jump-rope rhyme)

Spanish dancer do the splits,
Spanish dancer do high kicks;
Spanish dancer do the kangaroo,
Spanish dancer—out skidoo!

Tillie the Toiler sat on a boiler;
The boiler got hot,
Tillie got shot,
How many times did Tillie get shot?
One, two, three, etc.

Buster, Buster, climb the tree,
Buster, Buster, slap your knee;
Buster, Buster, throw a kiss,
Buster, Buster, do not miss.

Over the years, many children have enjoyed playing with paper dolls, acting out the behaviors and activities of daily life.

Scary stories offer another rite of passage. Being able to tell a frightening tale to younger children always proves how grown up you are by comparison, since displaying the courage to face a dark night, strange sounds, or unknown places is a sign of maturity. Some scary stories are told with a humorous ending or with a forced scare directed at one or two listeners, so that the others in the group laugh because the victim was caught off guard.

Babysitters are notoriously affected by nighttime's shivery trepidations. Being left to care for young children brings at once the thrill of responsibility and the fear of being alone and in charge. Although the stories stem from fears, they also serve to remind babysitters of the seriousness of their newfound maturity. Scary babysitter stories have entered the body of adolescent folklore that is passed along at pajama parties and campfires. I'm sure

DERISIVE RHYMES

In many cases rhymes that direct attention at one child are a form of teasing which offers nothing positive to the victim or the others hearing it. But many times these rhymes serve the purpose of pointing out expected norms. Enforcing concepts like cooperation, cleanliness, and loyalty give rise to a set of rhymes that persuade the victim to mend their ways. Here are three familiar examples:

Baby, baby, suck your thumb
Wash your face in bubble gum
Baby, baby, stick your head in gravy
Don't take it out until you join the Navy.

Tattletale, tattletale
Hanging on the bull's tail
When the bull has to pee
You will get a cup of tea.

I see London, I see France
I see someone's underpants
Not too big, not too small
Just the size of a cannonball.

Folklore is exchanged between children on the way to school, as well as in the classroom.

you've heard the story about the babysitter who kept getting threatening phone calls; turned out the murderer was calling from the upstairs phone. . . .

Summer camp provides yet another occasion for both the creation and transmission of children's folklore. Every summer, scores of parents send their offspring to camp, hoping to give them a special experience and an opportunity to learn more about "how to survive" in the world. Camps are almost always located in rural areas where stories of someone lurking in the nearby woods offer a plot for great nighttime tales that may also inspire the campers to more readily follow the rules. Sitting around a campfire telling scary tales or in bed at night whispering ghost stories is an experience most children have enjoyed (or maybe endured with chattering teeth).

Many times in horror stories that turn fun, younger children become the heroes. After attempts by parents and older siblings to save victims from some dire and dreadful mishap, these brave youths are able to thwart the scary villain. Older children's folklore may be full of modern stories like these—but their younger brothers and sisters could probably tell them that the theme is not a new one: in all good folktales, it's the youngest brother

who finds the treasure and the youngest sister who marries the prince.

Some stories work on the fears of those listening to the story, proving the courage and daring of the storyteller (at least to the storyteller's satisfaction). Sometimes all it takes to prove your own maturity and daring is to be able to startle your listeners. That's the purpose of the story that follows.

THERE was this guy who owned a creepy house with 140 rooms, and he also had a purple ape that weighed 999 pounds. The ape was 100 inches tall and 99 inches wide. The guy bragged and bragged to his friends about this ape, but all of his friends ignored him except one.

Best friends teach each other many things.

Children learn important lessons on the playground.

"If you want us to believe this ape story," he said, "I'll come see the ape and then everyone will know he is real."

So the friend went to this guy's house to see his ape, and he went to this ape's room. Sure enough, there was an ape. The ape gets up and starts chasing the guy all through every single room, and the guy gets very tired. So he sat down to rest by a table between two rooms, and all of a sudden . . . [the teller reaches out and tags a listener] . . . the ape says, "Tag, you're it."

SEXUAL information is very much a part of children's folklore. From things parents share to information learned from teachers, television, and friends, it all gets mixed together. Reaching adulthood is the ultimate goal, and in order to get there children need to know the facts. Things like child abuse, moral issues, abortion, and even the fear of sexually transmitted diseases become a part of children's lore. Many times the issues are touched on with humor, even **derisive** humor if necessary, to help ease the anxiety felt by youths when dealing with sensitive topics.

Whatever the rhyme or song and however they go about sharing it, the business of growing up is one of the most important in a child's life. Folklore author Simon J. Bonner says that for children, reaching adulthood is more important many times than understanding it—and children seem to constantly push each other toward adulthood. Those who prove they are the most mature can become the heroes of their group.

Tea parties teach children how to get along with others.

FOUR

Learning to Get Along with Others
Folklore That Reinforces Social Skills

Children's folklore provides them with guidelines for interacting.

PARENTS AND teachers may set standards for conduct in the home and at school, but children then work with this basic framework to create their own formula for how to get along on the playground and on the street. How to act in particular circumstances and how to recognize another child who has not learned these skills are insights often seen in the stories of earlier generations.

ONCE there lived a rich merchant who hosted a children's party. Among the guests were the children of some very rich and important people. The merchant himself was very learned. He had gone to college and was clever, but he also had a heart. Of course he was spoken of more for his money than his open nature. His home was the stopping place of the rich, the important, and many others who needed a place to stay.

The children at the party were talking to each other as they do, children's prattle, when a girl who was very beautiful and very proud began to speak. "I am a child of the court and am well-born and no one who is not well-born can rise in the world." In truth, her father was Groom of the Chambers, which was a high office at court. But this child who had been doted on by the servants who cared for her should have realized that no one can help her birth.

Instead of demonstrating proper humility, she continued, "And those whose names end with 'sen' can never be anything at all. Even if they study and read and work hard, they will never be

One of the important lessons siblings learn from one another is how to live closely with another person.

anyone. We mustn't let anyone with these last names play with us."

The daughter of the merchant did not like this speech at all, since her father's name was Petersen. "My papa can buy a hundred dollars' worth of bonbons to give away to children," she said. "Can your father do that?"

Another little girl whose father was editor of the newspaper told the gathering of children that her father could write about everyone else's father in the paper and for that many men were afraid of him. This child also looked proud, as if she were a real princess.

Now while all this talk was going on, a boy was looking in at the party from a door that stood slightly ajar. He was a poor boy, so poor that he was not even allowed to enter the room. The cook had given him permission to look in at the well-dressed children, which was a great treat for him. "I wish I could be one of them," he whispered.

But when he heard what was said about the

Pretty much all the honest truth telling in the world is done by children.

—*Oliver Wendell Holmes*

Good friends are sometimes hard to find. Recognizing the character of a good friend and learning to be one are important steps in socialization.

Two friends were traveling together when a bear suddenly appeared. The first friend ran for a tree at the side of the road, and climbed into the branches before the bear could see him. The second friend could not climb so easily, and he was not able to get away from the bear. Thinking quickly, he threw himself on the ground and pretended to be dead. The bear walked all around him, sniffing and sniffing. The man remained very still, holding his breath, for he had heard that a bear will not touch a dead body. The bear pressed his mouth to his ear and whispered something, and then left without harming him.

The first friend came down from the tree and asked what the bear had whispered to him when he put his mouth in his ear. The second friend replied, "He told me not to travel with a friend who deserts you at the first sign of danger."

Moral: Misfortune tests the sincerity of friendship.

Playing with a wagon is a valuable lesson in taking turns and sharing resources.

Computers offer children new opportunities for learning about the world and sharing.

names, he was very unhappy for his last name ended in 'sen.' His parents were too poor to even buy a newspaper, and now he knew he would never turn out well. He was born this way and he might as well be content.

Many years later, when the children had become grown-ups themselves, there stood a wonderful house in the town. It was beautifully furnished and everyone admired it as they passed by or visited. They wondered who lived in the house. Who of those children that listened and participated in children's prattle that day called this house his home?

It was the poor boy. He had indeed become someone great even though his name ended in "sen."

THIS moralistic folktale teaches children about the worth of all individuals, an important realization for getting along with others. Although children often squabble, basically, they work hard at maintaining their relationships with their friends. As we discussed earlier, belonging to a group and feeling wanted is important to everyone and especially to children. Children's folklore provides them with guidelines for complying with what the group considers to be acceptable behavior.

The security of having friends is so strong an influence, in fact, that sometimes children will bend their family's rules and morals to become a part of a group. No mater what kids think, however, there is no escaping social rules; groups of children or adolescents have rules of their own. These are not written down, but each member knows his or her place; they all know how they need to dress, wear their hair, and behave to remain a member.

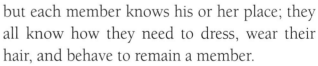

Not long ago, a group of my daughter's friends gathered at our house for an evening of games. As we sat around the table playing one of our favorite games of dominoes, these young teenagers threw sayings and remarks at each other as readily as they laid tiles onto the playing surface. At one point a boy set a domino in a place where one of the girls had been planning to play next. She looked at him and said,

Secret clubhouses often have their own rules.

"You did that on purpose. I bet you saw my tiles. Cheater, Cheater, Pumpkin Eater." The rest of the night when someone made a move another young person did not like, they were met with, "Cheater, Cheater, Pumpkin Eater."

I was startled to hear this form of folklore happening between teens, since I had assumed only younger children shared such quips and rhymes. Not only was I wrong, but I, too, found I enjoyed calling a young friend "Cheater, Cheater, Pumpkin Eater" when she took my spot on the playing board just as I was ready to lay down my last tile. Apparently, children's folklore never loses its value!

One of the most important lessons I learned that night with my daughter's friends was that they are able to cope with situations using their

Simple games give children guidelines for interacting with others.

When children play games together, one of the issues that must often be resolved is this: Who will be It? In order to settle this quickly and fairly, generations of children have passed along counting-out rhymes like these:

Wire, briar, limber, lock,
Three geese in a flock.
One flew east, one flew west,
One flew over the cuckoo's nest.
O-U-T, out goes you, you old dirty
Dishrag, you, out goes you.

Monkey, monkey, bottle of beer,
How many monkeys are there here?
One, two, three, out goes he (she).

The people who live across the way,
At 19-18 East Broadway,
Every night they have a fight and
This is what they say:
Icky-bicky soda cracker,
Icky-bicky boo,
Icky-bicky soda cracker,
Out goes you.

Even the simplest games teach a sense of fair play.

own language. When someone crosses a line, whether it be cheating at a game or taunting someone with a fault, caution is given by using words they understand well but that allow a mixing of warning and humor.

Folklore often deals with the stresses of being a part of a social group. Who are the leaders? How do we choose to get along? What do we think of those in the group compared to those outside the group? Groups show loyalty to their peers and find ways to protect each other. Sometimes, when a member fails to comply with expectations, they turn against that person with insults that seem heartless and callous by adult standards. Being called a "mama's boy" or "teacher's pet" can be devastating for a child, because it evicts him from the children's group and sets him outside with the adults.

Taunts and teasing offer warning against unacceptable behaviors like cheating or tattling. Other warnings advise keeping your hands off of another child's possessions. And of course the perennial saying "Finders keepers, losers weepers" lets others know they better also keep track of their own things.

Sometimes children use games to resolve their differences. For instance, a brother said, "Okay, we'll play hoops. The winner gets to watch TV while the loser cuts the lawn." The same happens in the neighborhood. If one group of kids is trying to play on the seesaw at the playground and another tries to take over, one member might suggest a race to see who gains possession of the equipment.

Getting along with other is hard enough for adults; it's even more difficult for children who are still learning the social skills they'll need in life. Relationships between best friends, between siblings, and between playmates on the school playground are fraught with jealousy and rivalries. The world has limited resources, a painful lesson that children learn while sharing cookies and waiting for the ball. Games, stories, rhymes, and even insults offer children a folklore of social cues, an unwritten rulebook for getting along.

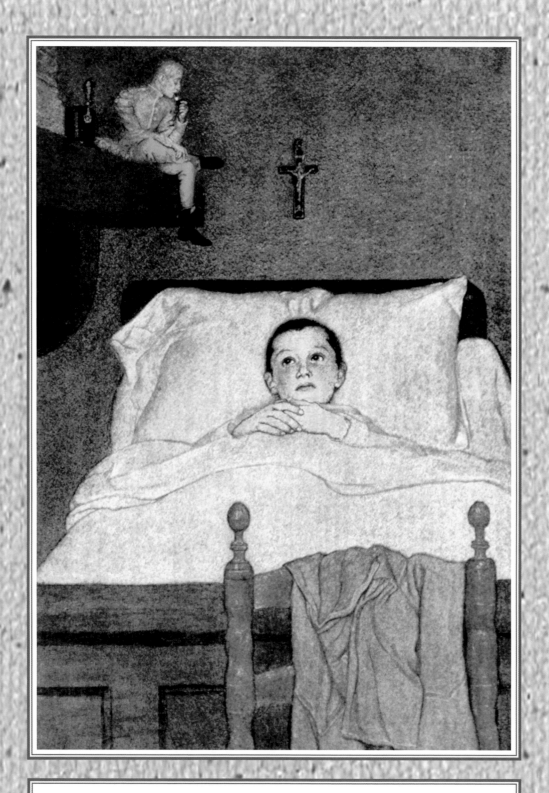

Children may use their imaginations for creating folklore that helps them cope with the adult world.

FIVE

Rights and Rebellion
Coping with the Adult World

Even long-ago children and adolescents occasionally rebelled against adult authority.

IN MANY WAYS children learn to follow the rules first and then they teach their version to those younger or lower in rank than themselves. Although they complain about following so many rules and mandates, they find their worlds also function better with them. They use many of the same ideas they learn from parents and teachers to work within their own groups. Very young children seldom venture far from the expectations of the adult world.

Once children approach the teen years, a transition from dependence on home and parents to independence is a natural development. At this time, boundaries are stretched, first in stories and eventually by stepping over the actual lines to test the truths behind the adult expectations. Children's folklore offers them a structure for doing this. If you're a child, it's not so scary to break the rules if you're doing it in a way that's acceptable according to the traditions of childhood.

Jokes and riddles are a fun form of folklore that children use mostly in a nondestructive way, to control their world. Laughter helps break the ice and eases some of the fears children deal with every day. Adults might consider some topics as inappropriate for jokes, but nothing is taboo for children. From embarrassing body noises to death and tragedy, children help each other cope through times of laughter. That laughter is itself a form of rebellion against the stuffy adult world.

A boy goes to school one day and his teacher gives him a homework assignment. He must write down three good words

Nonsense stories can offer children an escape from the grown-up world's pressures.

for school the next day. When he goes home he asks his sister, "Do you have any good words I can write?"

His sister says, "Shut up." So he writes it down.

Then he was listening to the radio and he hears someone say, "Yeah, yeah, yeah." So he writes that down.

Later while watching TV he sees Superman, so he writes that down.

The next day he goes to school. The teacher says, "Do you have any of the words from your homework assignment?"

The boy answers, "Shut up."

"Well," says the teacher, "Do you want to go to the principal's office?"

Not wanting to get in trouble, the boy looks down at his paper and reads the next words on his list: "Yeah, yeah, yeah."

The teacher sends him straight to the principal's office.

When the boy gets there, the principal asks him, "Who do you think you are?"

Desperate, the boy looks down at the last word on his list. He says, "Superman."

By telling each other nonsense stories like this, children can defy authority with fun and creativity. In a way they break the rules without getting in trouble. Teachers, parents, and others who spend so much time teaching and setting standards are put in the role of being controlled, embarrassed, and sometimes even eliminated. But once the joke is over, it is business as usual—doing homework, keeping curfews, and attending classes.

The modern folktales children tell each other may have to do with teachers and parents, but they are not so different from the old tales of witches and kings. Stories like "Hansel and Gretel" and "Jack in the Beanstalk" are about small people winning over big people, about children who triumph over evil authority figures. These childhood themes will never become outdated.

Children of every generation also long to belong to special groups, clubs that give them a sense of importance and belonging. These special societies may be as informal as a secret club that meets in the backyard or as formal as Scouts. Sometimes clubs demand that certain rights are required for membership. Rights are sometimes just an agreement to follow the rules of the group or they may include **initiation rituals**. These could include an obstacle course that must be completed—or maybe a set of objects that have to be collected. Even children in a tree fort may set up an initial quest that must be achieved for inclusion in their club. The Girl Scouts and Boy Scouts both hold initiation meetings where girls and boys agree to the Scout promise and laws. Agreeing to abide by these rules is a step toward maturity. It means that the

BOY SCOUT OATH OR PROMISE

On my honor, I will do my best
To do my duty to God and my country and to obey the
    Scout Law;
To help other people at all times;
To keep myself physically strong, mentally awake and
    morally straight.

child has accepted limitations and regulations as a necessary part of having fun together.

Still, children will continue to test boundaries in order to grow. Without these tests, children would be forever dependent on their parents' guidance; they would be unable to form their own system for making decisions.

Clearly, many traditional forms of rebellion are healthy for children on the road to becoming independent adults. But folklore also warns against rebellion's dangers. When we cross the boundary lines that protect our culture, we are on dangerous and uncertain ground. Children who no longer practice any of the rules or perform the basic courtesies they have been taught often believe they are too old, too smart, or too big to have to do what someone else tells them to. Old folktales let us know that there is nothing new about this behavior.

BOY SCOUT LAW

A Scout is:
    Trustworthy,
    Loyal,
    Helpful,
    Friendly,
    Courteous,
    Kind,
    Obedient,
    Cheerful,
    Thrifty,
    Brave,
    Clean,
    and Reverent.

GIRL SCOUT PROMISE

On my honor, I will try:
To serve God and my country,
To help people at all times,
And to live by the Girl Scout Law.

ONCE there was a merchant's daughter so kind and pretty everyone called her Beauty. She lived with her father and two sisters. They were quite wealthy until the merchant suffered financial losses and soon the family had nothing. The sisters just cried and complained while Beauty worked hard to comfort her father.

One day, word came that the lost merchant ship had arrived in the port. The father decided to meet the ship and before leaving, asked each daughter what she missed most about their old life; he would bring it back as a gift for each.

"Wonderful gowns," said the first daughter.

"A coach and four horses," said the second daughter.

But Beauty asked only for a rose because her garden was now filled with cabbages.

When the father met the ship he found the cargo spoiled and rotten. As he was returning home through a storm, tired and without money, he saw in the distance a large palace. When he

GIRL SCOUT LAW

I will do my best to be honest and fair, friendly and helpful, considerate and caring, courageous and strong, and responsible for what I say and do, and to respect myself and others, respect authority, use resources wisely, make the world a better place, and be a sister to every Girl Scout.

In many Slavic tales the heroine is aided by a doll, which is the East Slavic equivalent of the fairy godmother. The dolls help the child escape from situations that are harmful to the girl. Categorized as tales of initiation, the heroine performs certain tasks that allow her to mature along the way to her destination, which is usually marriage.

struggled to the door, it opened to a blazing fire and sumptuous meal. But there was no one around. After eating, he fell asleep.

In the morning he had dry garments but still saw no one in the house. Outside the door a fresh horse awaited him. As he went to leave he saw some roses and remembered Beauty's wish—but as soon as he had broken the stem, a beast came charging at him, accusing him of killing the rose.

"A rose that's cut can only die," the Beast roared. Reaching for his sword, he threatened the father's life.

"I have taken the rose for my daughter Beauty," the father begged.

"I will not take your life if one of your daughters willingly returns to the castle in your place."

The merchant could not agree to this, so he rode home to say good-bye to his children. But Beauty insisted she would go to the palace. After much argument, her father realized he could not keep her from the journey.

They arrived at the castle and saw the Beast at the far end of a corridor. After greeting one another, the Beast gave the father coins and jewels enough to restore his fortune. "Now be gone," said the Beast as he walked away. Father and daughter separated in tears.

Beauty began her life at the castle, and within a short time she realized she was not in any danger. Monkeys and a dog were dressed as court servants. A beautiful bird waited at her bedchamber, and she seemed to receive whatever she needed before she asked. She ate dinner with the Beast, enjoying his company.

Each night he said, "Beauty, will you marry me?" But she begged him not to ask that question.

Time went on in the same manner and Beauty was happy—except that each night before the Beast left her he asked if she would marry him. Finally, she told the Beast she could not marry him, but she would stay with him forever if he allowed her to go once to say good-bye to her father and family.

The Beast agreed but asked her to return before the moon was full. Then he gave her a golden ring. "When you are ready to come back, turn this ring three times around your finger and say aloud, 'I want to be in the palace of the Beast again.'"

As soon as the Beast finished his instructions, Beauty found herself in her father's home. Everything was as it had been when they were wealthy. Her family asked her many questions about the strange palace ruled by the Beast. Beauty tried to explain how she cared for the Beast, but they could not understand and the subject always returned to the events of the day.

Beauty's time with her family was filled with parties and young men, and she thought little of the Beast. One night she awoke from a dream of the palace. In the dream, she saw the Beast lying on the ground as if dead. She knew then she had met no one she cared for as she did the Beast.

Turning the ring, Beauty said aloud, "I want to be at the palace of the Beast!"

As she ran through the garden, she saw his still figure lying on the grass. Dropping to his side, she tried to talk to him. Finally the Beast opened his eyes, and she said, "Dearest Beast, I love you. I want to marry you."

As soon as the words were spoken, the Beast turned into a handsome young prince. He explained that he had been turned into a Beast by a fairy who was angry at the way he had cared only for appearances. Therefore he had become the ugliest Beast until he could be loved in spite of his appearance.

The entire castle celebrated the love of Beauty that night.

OLD folktales like this are cautionary tales for the next generation. They are like breadcrumbs left by a kind parent who longs for the child to find her way home. In this tale, both Beauty and the Beast traveled the difficult road toward independence—Beauty ventured outside her father's world with love and courage, while the Beast acted with a selfishness that was punished. Along the way each needed to learn important lessons about love and integrity.

Folktales may change their form somewhat from generation to generation, but the basic themes stay the same. Many children have to deal with "Beasts" in their lives, challenges like selfishness and pride, beauty or awkwardness, divorce or death. Some problems are self-inflicted and some come about through no fault of the children involved. But victories like those in Beauty and the Beast show children that adulthood can be achieved with triumph and joy.

Children have always sought safety and predictability.

SIX

Coping with
the Unknown
Controlling the World
with Words

The world outside the home can look threatening to a child.

ILLNESSES AND death are often difficult for children to deal with because they cannot see the reason these things happen. They like life to be predictable and safe—and things that upset that safety are frightening.

Once my daughter planned for months to attend a rabbit show sponsored by the rabbit club to which she belonged. She baked cookies and made rabbit lollypops for the group to sell to help support the club. She had special bunnies of her own she would enter and promised to work in the kitchen on the day of the show, serving breakfast and lunch. She was counting the days until the show—but the night before, she developed a stomach virus that kept her up all night and left her with a fever the day of the show.

At one point during the night while I tried to comfort her, she said to me, "Why did it have to be *this* night?"

Some questions have no answers. Adults still struggle with this sad fact. One way that children cope with life's unpredictability is by structuring life's bumps with rhymes.

Mother, mother I am ill.
Send for the doctor
Over the hill.
First comes the doctor,
Then comes the nurse,
Then comes the lady
With the alligator purse.
Didn't like the doctor,

Didn't like the nurse.
Didn't like the lady
With the alligator purse.
Out went the doctor,
Out went the nurse.
Out went the lady
With the alligator purse.

Sickness and disappointment are unavoidable in the lives of children. To add to their stress, adults are constantly confronting them with the pressures of the future by asking questions like, "What do you want to be when you grow up?" When looking ahead at the future's uncertainties, children play with ways of predicting the answers. As we mentioned earlier, even jump-rope and ball-bouncing rhymes predict who the child will marry, how many children they will have, and even where they might live. Children and young teens may also turn to other superstitions to help them catch a glimpse of the future.

For instance, you probably already know that daisies are useful flowers, good for predicting the sentiments of a special member of the opposite sex. Almost all of us have said, "He loves me, he loves me not" (or "She loves me, she loves me not") at one time or another in our lives.

Adolescents have their own folklore that provides them with a structure for anticipating adulthood.

Names also carry hidden meanings. One way of telling if a couple are "meant" for each other is to write their names side-by-side; then cross out the letters that the two names have in common. Saying the  words, "Friendship, courtship, love, hatred, marriage," count off the remaining letters; whatever word is said last predicts the true state of romance between these two individuals.

Another count and cross-out *oracle* is based on words arranged in this pattern:

L	M	D	H	E
O	A	I	A	N
V	R	V	T	G
E	R	O	E	A
	Y	R		G
		C		E
		E		

One person chooses a number—for example, five—and her friend goes through the words one by one, crossing out each fifth letter. On subsequent rounds, she skips the letters that are already crossed out, until one word is completely gone. Whichever word is gone first indicates the first thing that will happen to the person. Of course, in some cases, the word divorce will be the first crossed out, and it's a bit difficult to get divorced if you've never been married. The future, however, as every child knows, is a mysterious and nonsensical place.

All manner of ordinary objects can be used for foretelling the events of adulthood. If you blow on dandelions that have gone to seed, the number of seeds that remain stuck to the stem indicates how many children you will one day have. When dandelions aren't in season, the number of flips back and forth that it takes to break a soda tab will tell you the same thing. (So much for zero-population growth!) If you've tried the oracles of true love already listed above and you still have your doubts, you might want to try twisting the stem of an apple while saying the alphabet. Whatever letter you say as the stem breaks is the initial of the person you will marry. Apple seeds are also useful for determining the state of your own heart as well as your prospective sweetheart's. Count the seeds while saying this rhyme:

One I love, two I love, three I love, I say.
Four I love with all my heart,
Five I'll cast away.
Six he loves, seven she loves,

Historically, stories have also helped children cope with the world. For instance, fairy tales are filled with young children who have lost one or both parents, usually the mother. This is probably based on historical fact; since an enormous percentage of women died during childbirth up until the beginning of the 20th century, many children did indeed face life without a mother. And, of course, this led in many cases to the remarriage of the father and the stepmother.

Eight they both love.
Nine he comes, ten he tarries,
Eleven he courts, twelve he marries.

If there are more than 12 seeds, simply start over.

   For generations, one of the favorite oracle activities on school buses and playgrounds has been the paper fortuneteller. Chances are you don't need me to explain what this is. In case you've forgotten, if you fold a piece of paper in a certain way, you end up with a pocket that opens and closes around eight triangles. Un-

Even building a snowman has its own traditions and folklore.

der the flap of each triangle, you write a "fortune." Here are just a few possibilities:

You will be rich.
You will marry someone with lots of money.
You will break your leg.
Your husband/wife will be ugly.
You will be poor.
You will be a movie star.
You will get sick and die.
You will drive a limousine.

Almost anything will do, but it's always nice to have a good mix of "bad" and "good" fortunes. Then you close the flaps and write a number on the outside of the triangle, and on outer squares you write the name of a color. Whoever wants their fortune told must choose one of the colors, and with your thumbs and forefingers inside the flap, you then make the pocket wink open and shut, spelling out the color. It will end up with a number revealed, which must then be counted as the fortuneteller again opens and shuts the pocket. This can be done several times, but three is usually the accepted number. On the final count, the triangle is opened, revealing the person's fortune.

Children don't really believe these predictions. They know that each time they do one of these activities, something different will be predicted. However, these activities give them a way to think about the future within a secure framework. They give

children a sense of control over what can't be controlled. So important is this to them that they will even predict silly things—like holding a buttercup under a friend's chin to determine if that person likes butter.

Children's folklore also helps them to begin thinking about consequences. If you do one thing, something else happens; understanding this concept is a life-long lesson. In a complex world, the precise consequences of actions are sometimes difficult to unravel. Children have various superstitions that make the world seem a bit more predictable, as though it were governed by a prescribed list of rules and consequences:

Step on the line, break your spine.
Step on a crack, break your mother's back.
If you open an umbrella in the house, you'll have bad luck.
If you see a ladybug, you'll have good luck.
If you find a penny on the ground, that's good luck.
Finding a penny minted the year you were born is even better
   luck.
If your hand itches, you're getting some money.
If your nose itches, you're going to kiss a fool.
If your right ear burns, someone is talking good about you.
If you right ear burns, someone is speaking ill of you.
If you kill a daddy-longlegs, it will rain.
If a toad pees on you, you'll get warts.
If you kiss your elbow, you'll turn into a person of the opposite
   sex.

As children move into the new worlds of middle school and high school, autographs in yearbooks provide a way to share memories with friends. Earlier generations used autograph al-

AUTOGRAPH VERSES

In Germany, during the 15th century, university students collected signatures from their professors. These signatures then served as letters of introduction when they applied for jobs.

Victorians signed autograph albums as a sign of class. Often very elaborate penmanship and artwork adorned these collections and could include sentiments or poetry. Valentines became a popular vehicle for these verses.

Some of the sentiments offered made little sense, as in the following little verse:

Playmate, I cannot play with you
My dolly has the flu
Boo hoo hoo hoo hoo hoo
Ain't got no rain barrel
Ain't got no cellar door
But we'll be jolly friends
Forever more.

bums for the same purpose. Besides the keepsake quality of the books, these also serve to prod the young person along toward the next academic year. For generations, the same ditties have been written on these occasions.

Remember Grant
Remember Lee
The heck with them
Remember me.

Or:

UR 2 good 2 be 4 gotten.

Surrounded by adults who are always listening to make sure children are "being good," children of all ages often enjoy secret languages. These allow children the opportunity to communicate in the presence of others, especially adults, without others understanding their communication. The feeling of power and mystery is worth expending many hours and great effort to practice and perfect this new language. Many such languages have been used by children over the years including pig Latin, bop talk, G-talk, ubbie-dubbie, and egg talk.

Folk traditions allow children to manipulate language and words to help them cope with the ordinary stresses of daily life. Helpful adults may try to spoon-feed the "right" answers to children, but children long to figure out the world for themselves. When they feel they have come to a satisfactory solution on their own, they are one step further on their way to adulthood.

This child knew much of the same folklore that you do today.

SEVEN

Tomorrow's Parents
Linking the Generations

A sense of stability is important to a child's well-being—but he may possess great strength for helping to create that sense of stability.

ALONG TIME AGO, way down in the South, when birds didn't have comfy nests of their own, a wonderful nesting tree grew up out of nowhere. It was big, and round, and already full of every kind of nest a bird would ever want. Nests were everywhere just waiting for birds to come and pick them. There was also a sign at the base of the tree that said, "First to come, First to choose."

Old Buzzard was one of the first to see the sign. He looked over all the nests and then said, "No, thank you. None suit me!"

Even the softest, prettiest nest wasn't good enough for him. The other birds couldn't believe he was being so uppity.

When Hummingbird zipped into the tree to choose her nest, Old Buzzard just laughed. Then Oriole came to choose one and Old Buzzard said, "That's the funniest nest I ever saw!"

Oriole loved the nest, though, and took it anyway. Old Buzzard made the same comments when Thrush and Mockingbird picked their nests.

"Hey, Mockingbird, that nest looks like a bundle of sticks," Old Buzzard said with a laugh.

But Mockingbird did not care what he thought. She flew away with her nest and made it into a wonderful home for her family.

Soon all the birds looked at Old Buzzard. All the nests were gone. He was so persnickety that he had no nest at all. Old Buzzard felt really bad now, but he pretended not to. Instead, he hopped over to a fence and sat right down. And to this day that's where you'll see Old Buzzard, either sitting on the fence or a-floating in the sky with no place to call home.

THIS African American children's tale communicates the concept that home and stability are important. Birds choose homes and make places where they can raise their young so they are safe from predators. The nests are also havens where their young are able to learn what they need before "leaving the nest." Every year a phoebe builds a nest on the cross beams of my front porch. From past experience, she knows that first her eggs and then her babies will be safe and warm there, able to mature into self-reliant adults. She's done by instinct year after year what humans also long to do for their children: create a secure and nurturing environment.

In today's world, children are often perceived as innocent and helpless, needing the protection and guidance of adults if they are to thrive. And it's true, of course, that children grow better, emotionally, intellectually, and physically, when they're raised in homes where they are safe and loved. Sometimes, however, adults fail to recognize the strength that children possess.

Whether they are sharing words or rhymes, playing games, telling each other stories, or singing silly songs, children have immense power to shape their worlds. They manipulate their peers and entertain adults, they share endearments and threaten each

. . . The rules of the game of marbles are handed down, just like so-called moral realities, from one generation to the next, and are preserved solely by the respect that is felt for them by individuals. . . . The little boys . . . are gradually trained by the older ones in respect for the law; and in any case they aspire from their hearts to the virtue. . . . If this is not "morality," then where does morality begin?

—Jean Piaget, *The Moral Judgment of a Child*

For generations, camping out has been a favorite childhood activity.

According to childhood folklore, you can hear the ocean roaring inside a seashell.

Whether it be useful or silly, true or false, folklore connects us to the past and to each other, because it requires face-to-face contact. It exists when people share an identity, when they recognize themselves as a member of a group united by race, nationality, occupation, class, geography, or age; and since all of us once belonged to the group of human beings we call children, the folklore of childhood brings together all of us.

—Mary and Herbert Knapp, *One Potato, Two Potato*

other with insults, and they create a world where they understand one another in much the same way that adults do in their world. As children grow older, childish folklore will be replaced with the folklore of the larger community, the workplace, and perhaps the church.

And then one day, children will find "nests" of their own, safe places where the next generation can grow. Each time they

The story of Little Red Riding Hood is horrifying and yet reassuring to children.

For years, **theologians**, teachers, and psychologists have debated the positive or negative effects of fairy tales on children. They wonder if the cruelty, violence, and superstition found in the tales is detrimental to children's development. Some of these debates began as long ago as the 17th century when these stories were first written down. But the one thing that cannot be argued or debated is the lasting quality of the tales. The popularity of Disney's movie versions of these tales attests to their enduring power.

Some child development experts believe that children who hear about the "bad guys" in folk tales then have the opportunity to recognize a part of themselves. Characters in these stories are many times one-dimensional; although they are perceived as bad, that wickedness usually embodies only one bad trait, like envy or greed or gluttony. Defining this trait in someone outside themselves allows children to recognize it in themselves as well.

This child is creating a collection of folklore she will pass on to her children.

sing a lullaby or tell a story, each time they play peek-a-boo or teach the alphabet song, they will find themselves passing along a type of folklore they may have forgotten—children's folklore. The act of transmitting this folklore links the generations together.

Of course these children's children won't be like baby birds, waiting passively to have their open mouths stuffed full of lore. Instead, they'll soon be grabbing their traditions from other children, playing their folklore on the playground, in the backyard, and on the school bus. They'll create their own world with its own rules, a structured place where they can grow toward adulthood.

And then one day they'll have children of their own. . . .

Further Reading

Bronner, Simon J. *American Children's Folklore: A Book of Rhymes, Games, Jokes, Stories, Secret Languages, Beliefs and Camp Legends.* Little Rock, Ark.: August House, 1988.

Cashdan, Sheldon. *The Witch Must Die: How Fairy Tales Shape Our Lives.* New York: Basic Books, 1999.

Emrich, Duncan. *Folklore on the American Land.* Boston: Little, Brown and Company, 1972.

Tatar, Maria. *Off With Their Heads.* Princeton, N.J.: Princeton University Press, 1992.

Zeitlin, Steven J., Amy J. Kotkin, and Holly Cutting Baker. *A Celebration of American Family Folk Lore.* New York: Pantheon Books, 1982.

For More Information

Aaron Shepard's Home Page
www.aaronshep.com/stories/

American Folklore
americanfolklore.net/folktales/

Children's Folklore
ausis.gf.vu.lt/eka/childfolk/teasing.html

Folk and Fairy Tales
www.pitt.edu/~dash/folklinks.html

Story Lore
tech-head.com/story.htm

Glossary

Derisive Expressing ridicule or scorn.

Ethical Having to do with what is right and wrong.

Folklorists People who study folklore as a research subject.

Initiation rituals Ceremonies or ordeals that must be performed or endured before a person can enter a society or club.

Norm That which is standard or acceptable.

Oracle Something that foretells the future.

Parody A song, story, or rhyme that pokes fun of a more serious work by mimicking it in a foolish or sarcastic way.

Philosophy Way of thinking about something.

Prejudices Biases; dislikes that are not based on reasonable grounds.

Rites of passage Ceremonies or activities that demonstrate a person's entrance into a new stage of life; bar mitzvahs, graduation, and First Communion are examples.

Taboo Something that is not allowed.

Theologians People who study ideas about God.

Index

Biographies

Sherry Bonnice lives in a log cabin on a dirt road in Montrose, Pennsylvania, with her husband, teenage daughter, five dogs, and 25 rabbits. She loves homeschooling her daughter, reading, and making quilts. Sherry has spent the last two years coediting three quilt magazines and writing a quilt book. Writing books for children and young people has been her dream.

Dr. Alan Jabbour is a folklorist who served as the founding director of the American Folklife Center at the Library of Congress from 1976 to 1999. Previously, he began the grant-giving program in folk arts at the National Endowment for the Arts (1974–76). A native of Jacksonville, Florida, he was trained at the University of Miami (B.A.) and Duke University (M.A., Ph.D.). A violinist from childhood on, he documented old-time fiddling in the Upper South in the 1960s and 1970s. A specialist in instrumental folk music, he is known as a fiddler himself, an art he acquired directly from elderly fiddlers in North Carolina, Virginia, and West Virginia. He has taught folklore and folk music at UCLA and the University of Maryland and has published widely in the field.